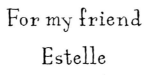

For my friend
Estelle

First U.S. edition 2005

Library of Congress Cataloging-in-Publication Data is available.

Library of Congress Catalog Card Number 2005046927

ISBN 0-7636-2671-6

2 4 6 8 10 9 7 5 3 1

Printed in China

This book was typeset in Aunt Mildred.
The illustrations were done in oil.

Candlewick Press
2067 Massachusetts Avenue
Cambridge, Massachusetts 02140

visit us at www.candlewick.com

Santasaurus

Niamh Sharkey

CANDLEWICK PRESS

CAMBRIDGE, MASSACHUSETTS

Wen the snow began to fall before Christmas,
Ollie, Molly, and Milo wrote letters
to Santasaurus.

Ollie wished for
a dinobot.

Molly wished for a dinocycle.

All Milo wanted was to meet
Santasaurus and to fly
in his sleigh.

When the cold wind blew

through Dinosaur Town,

Ollie, Molly, and Milo went

Christmas shopping with Momosaurus.

"What hustle and bustle and squoosh!"

said Momosaurus.

Later, Momosaurus, Dadosaurus,
Ollie, Molly, and Milo
wrapped presents
in fancy paper,

hung up
paper chains,

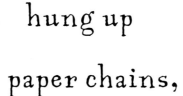

turned on

the lights,

strung popcorn to hang on the tree,

and baked sugarplum cakes

for everyone.

It's Christmas Eve!

Everything is ready for the Dinosaurs' Christmas.
Ollie, Molly, and Milo hang up their stockings
and leave milk and cookies for Santasaurus
and carrots for the dinodeer.

Soon everyone

is sleeping . . .

except Milo.

Listen! What's that?
Is it the sound of
sleigh bells ringing?

Milo pops out
from under the covers and
creeps ever so quietly down the stairs.

 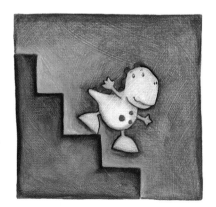 

Who is standing by the Christmas tree?

SANTASAURUS!

In the blink of a magic eye,

Milo and Santasaurus

shot up the chimney

to the sleigh on the roof.

They flew up from the house . . .

and over Dinosaur Town.

They delivered presents to dinosaur children

all over Dinosaur World.

It was still dark when Santasaurus
brought Milo home.

"Good night, dinodeer!" Milo said,
giving each one a carrot.

"Good night, Santasaurus,
and thank you for the sleigh ride!"
Milo was back in bed and
fast asleep before you could say
"plum pudding."

"Hooray!" shouted Molly.
"It's Christmas morning!"

Ollie's best present
was a cool dinobot!

Molly got
a fantastic dinocycle!

And Milo?

Milo got a miniature sleigh,

eight little dinodeer, and a Christmas hat

just like the one Santasaurus wore!

So, were all the dinosaurs happy?
Yesosaurus, they were!
Merry Christmas,
Ollie, Molly, and Milo!

Merry Christmas,
Momosaurus and Dadosaurus!
HAPPY DINOSAURS' CHRISTMAS!